# Flash Flood!

Story by Sally Cowan

Illustrations by Alisha Monnin

## Contents

| | | |
|---|---|---|
| Chapter 1 | Heavy Rain | **2** |
| Chapter 2 | Unloading the Sandbags | **6** |
| Chapter 3 | Helicopters in the Valley | **12** |
| Chapter 4 | The Emergency Centre | **18** |
| Chapter 5 | The Floodwaters Recede | **24** |
| Chapter 6 | The Most Important Thing | **28** |

## Chapter 1

# Heavy Rain

Dani woke up during the night to the sound of rain. Normally, she liked the sound of rain falling on the roof, but this was different. The rain was much heavier than usual. Dani was worried. Tomorrow was the school fair.

Despite the rain, Dani must have gone back to sleep, as she woke up suddenly to the sound of her alarm. She was looking forward to seeing her friend Zoey at the fair. There was no sound of rain on the roof any more, but when Dani looked out her bedroom window, she got a horrible shock. Water was pouring down the gutters of the street outside her house. Some huge puddles were forming around the drains, which were blocked with leaves and branches.

Dani rushed to wake her parents. "Mum and Dad, look out the window!" she exclaimed.

As Mum looked out, she grabbed her phone to check the news. "There's a flash flood warning!" she said.

"What's a flash flood?" asked Dani. The water didn't look very flashy or shiny to her.

"It's when a lot of rain falls very quickly," replied Mum. "There's too much water to soak into the ground, so it stays on the surface and causes a flood."

"There must have been a huge amount of rain," said Dad, frowning. "And from the look of those grey clouds, there's still more to come."

"But we have to go to the school fair!" said Dani, unhappily. "I'm meeting Zoey there."

## Chapter 2

# Unloading the Sandbags

Just then, Mum's phone pinged. It was a message from Dani's school:

*The school fair is cancelled. Main Street is closed. The emergency services website advises everyone in this area to stay indoors. People living in the low-lying valley should consider leaving their homes if it is safe to do so. We are using the school hall as an emergency centre for anyone affected by the floodwaters.*

"I hope Zoey's all right," said Dani. "She lives in the valley!"

"Yes, it might be a lot worse down there," said Mum. "The water will be flowing into the valley and filling up the river. I'll give Jason a call to check on them."

Jason was Zoey's dad. He and Zoey lived in a house near the river with their dog, Pom-pom. Mum called Jason, but he didn't answer. She tried sending a text message instead.

"The text didn't go through," said Mum.

"There's a rescue hotline number," said Dad, looking at his phone. "I'll call that. They should be able to check on Jason and Zoey."

As Dani ate breakfast, there was a loud knock at the door. Some emergency workers were delivering sandbags from a large truck. They were asking residents to place the sandbags outside their houses, around doorways and windows, to stop water from getting inside.

"You're on higher ground here," said one of the workers, "so you've still got time to prepare. There was about 150 millimetres of rain overnight. It took everyone by surprise, even the weather forecasters!"

Dani watched as the workers helped Mum and Dad move sandbags from the truck to the front door. She started to feel a bit sick in her stomach.

"Are we safe?" she asked the worker.

"Yes," he said, with a kind smile. "But please don't walk anywhere, or go in a car, because many roads are underwater. It can be hard to tell how deep the floodwaters are. People and cars can be swept away in the fast-moving water, so it's much too dangerous to stay outside."

The workers drove the truck to the next house. Dad went to help their neighbour Mr Karim. He was elderly, and couldn’t handle the heavy sandbags by himself.

“What can I do to help, Mum?” asked Dani, back inside the house.

“Let’s roll up this rug and carry it upstairs,” replied Mum.

“Okay,” said Dani. “I can pick up any other things that are on the floor, or low down, and take them upstairs, too. If any water gets in, at least we can keep these things dry.”

“Great idea, Dani!” said Mum.

## Chapter 3

# Helicopters in the Valley

Dani spent an hour moving cushions, books, photos and sports equipment upstairs. Meanwhile, the rain had started again. When Dani stopped to look out an upstairs window, she began to feel quite worried. The water was rising, and the street was looking more and more like a river.

Dani had never seen a flood in person. Sometimes she'd seen floods on the news and thought it might be fun to go paddling around the streets in a canoe, or to play in the water. Now, she realised why that was a terrible idea! The water was not nice and clear, like in the river or the local swimming pool. It was muddy and dirty, and there were pieces of rubbish floating down the street. Dani even noticed Mr Karim's garden chairs floating in their backyard. A flood was a serious problem!

Then, Dani heard helicopters in the distance. She peered out the window again and saw the helicopters flying over the valley, near Zoey's neighbourhood!

Dani raced downstairs. Dad was in the kitchen, moving tins and packets of food to the higher cupboards. Mum was taking down the curtains in the living room.

"There are helicopters down near Zoey's house!" cried Dani. "Mum, can you please call Zoey's dad again?"

Mum tried calling Jason, but there was still no response.

"Oh, dear," said Mum, looking at her phone. "People are being rescued from the valley. It's on the news. The river has overflowed its banks and Valley Bridge is badly damaged."

"I hope Zoey is all right," said Dani. A feeling of panic was rising in her throat. "Will *we* have to be rescued?"

"I hope not, Dani," said Mum. "Our instructions are to stay put! Remember what the emergency worker said? Let's just hope that the rain stops soon."

"Let's all take a few deep breaths," said Dad, calmly. "Worrying won't help anyone."

Dani knew Dad was right, but the sight of the helicopters was quite alarming. After taking a few breaths, Dani did feel a bit better. But she couldn't stop thinking about Zoey.

## Chapter 4

# The Emergency Centre

Dani and her parents managed to sleep that night. The rain stopped, and the sandbags kept the water out of their house. By the morning, the floodwaters had receded enough that it was safe to go outside. Dad went to see if Mr Karim needed any help, while Mum checked her phone. There were still no messages from Zoey's dad.

"I've volunteered to help at the emergency centre in the school hall," Mum said to Dani. "Come on, the coordinator said she can find a job for you, too."

Dani and Mum pulled on their gumboots and trudged along the muddy streets towards the school hall. They passed piles of rubbish strewn about in the mud. There were cars stranded in an enormous puddle in the supermarket car park.

"A flash flood can do a lot of damage," said Dani. "I hope this won't ever happen again!"

"Unfortunately, it might," said Mum. "Climate change is making extreme weather events like this more common."

Dani knew about climate change, and now its effects were in her own neighbourhood.

When they arrived at the hall, the school fair decorations were still up on the walls. But instead of fair stalls, Dani was amazed to see rows of camp beds. The people whose homes had been flooded were trying to get some rest.

"Come on, Dani," said Mum. "Let's see what we can do."

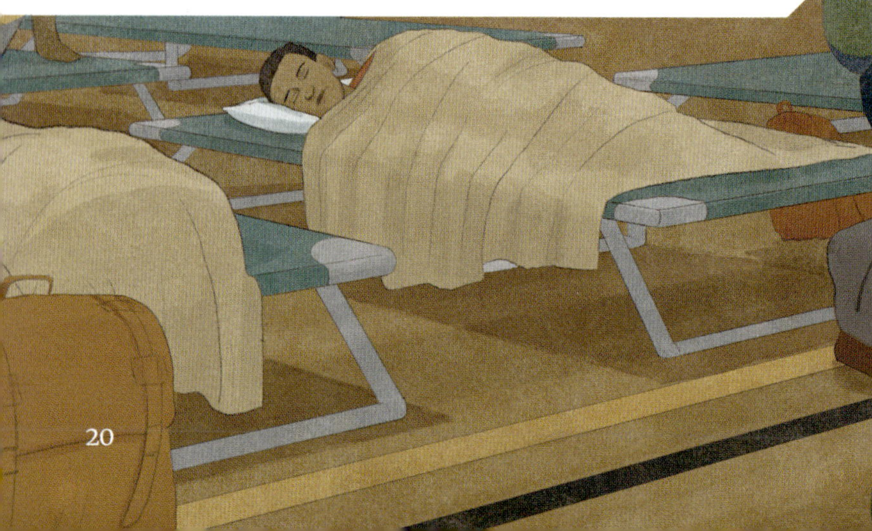

SIGN
IN
HERE

Just then, someone called out, “Dani!”

It was Zoey!

“Thank goodness you’re safe!” said Dani, rushing to hug her friend. “I was so worried when your dad didn’t reply to Mum’s messages.”

"Our house got flooded," said Zoey, sadly. "The power went out and Dad's phone battery died, so he couldn't use his phone. It all happened so quickly! We had to climb up onto the roof to be rescued. I got pulled up into a helicopter, but …" Zoey burst into tears.

"What's wrong?" asked Dani.

"I don't know what happened to Pom-pom," cried Zoey, wiping tears from her cheeks. "He was right behind me when Dad helped me up onto the roof. But when I went to grab Pom-pom, he had disappeared."

Chapter 5

# The Floodwaters Recede

Mum invited Zoey and her dad to stay in the spare room at Dani's house. Dani was happy to have her friend stay with her, but she had never seen Zoey so upset.

There was no school for the week because the area was badly affected by the flash flooding. So, the girls spent a lot of time in Dani's room, reading and listening to music. Dani tried to cheer her friend up by lending Zoey some of her favourite clothes. But Zoey stayed very quiet.

The floodwaters were receding from the houses in the valley. At the emergency centre, Mum had been organising teams of volunteers to help clean up people's homes. One day, Dani and Zoey went with Mum, Dad, Jason and one of the teams to check Zoey's house. It was a muddy mess, inside and outside. Dani felt so sad and sorry for Zoey and her dad, because all their furniture and belongings had been damaged by the floodwater.

"We'll be able to clean the house up, but it's going to take a lot of effort," said Jason.

Dani grabbed one of the shovels. "I'm ready to get started!" she said.

"Excellent!" said Mum. "Why don't you girls start by shovelling the mud out of Zoey's bedroom?"

In her bedroom, Zoey found a soggy, mud-stained cushion. "This is Pom-pom's bed," she said, glumly.

Dani gave her friend a big hug. It really was heartbreaking thinking about poor Pom-pom.

Chapter 6

# The Most Important Thing

Back at Dani's house that afternoon, the girls snuggled under blankets on the couch.

"Here, this should warm you up," said Dad, bringing them hot chocolate drinks with marshmallows. "You are both incredible workers! With you two to help, we'll have your house as good as new in no time, Zoey."

Zoey could barely smile. She hadn't smiled properly since Dani had found her in the emergency centre.

There was a knock at the door, and Mum answered. A rescue worker came into the living room holding a rolled-up blanket.

"Which one of you is Zoey?" she said to the girls. "I've got a little friend who wants to see her."

Just then, a furry head popped out of the blanket.

"Pom-pom!" shouted Zoey. She jumped off the couch and took Pop-pom from the rescue worker, cradling him in her arms.

"Pom-pom is a resilient little dog!" said the rescue worker. "I was out in a rescue boat and saw him swimming in the floodwaters. I picked him up and took him to the animal shelter. Luckily, you'd listed Pom-pom as missing, so we could get him back to you!"

"Thank you so much!" said Zoey, as Pom-pom wriggled around excitedly, trying to lick her chin.

"The vet at the shelter examined Pom-pom," said the rescue worker. "He was very tired from all that swimming, and he's rather dirty, but otherwise unhurt!"

That afternoon, Dani and Zoey gave Pom-pom a bath and dried his fur.

"I know how awful it must be to have lost all your belongings, Zoey," said Dani. "But the most important thing is that Pom-pom is alive and well."

Zoey gave Pom-pom a hug and looked at Dani. Dani thought she had never seen her friend smile so happily!